This is a fictionalised biography describing some of the key moments (so far!) in the career of Bernardo Silva.

Some of the events described in this book are based upon the author's imagination and are probably not entirely accurate representations of what actually happened.

Tales from the Pitch
Bernardo Silva
by Harry Coninx

Published by Raven Books
An imprint of Ransom Publishing Ltd.
Unit 7, Brocklands Farm, West Meon, Hampshire GU32 1JN, UK
www.ransom.co.uk

ISBN   978 180047 804 6
First published in 2023
Second edition published 2024
Reprinted 2024

Copyright © 2024 Ransom Publishing Ltd.
Text copyright © 2024 Ransom Publishing Ltd.
Cover illustration by Ben Farr © 2024 Ben Farr

A CIP catalogue record of this book is available from the British Library.

All rights reserved. No part of this publication may be reproduced, stored in a retrieval system, or transmitted, in any form or by any means, electronic, mechanical, photocopying, recording or otherwise, without the prior permission of the publishers.

There is a reading comprehension quiz available for this book in the popular Accelerated Reader® software system. For information about ATOS, Accelerated Reader, quiz points and reading levels please visit www.renaissance.com. Accelerated Reader, AR, the Accelerated Reader Logo, and ATOS are trademarks of Renaissance Learning, Inc. and its subsidiaries, registered common law or applied for in the U.S. and other countries. Used under license.

The rights of Harry Coninx to be identified as the author and of Ben Farr to be identified as the illustrator of this Work have been asserted by them in accordance with sections 77 and 78 of the Copyright, Design and Patents Act 1988.

TALES FROM THE PITCH

BERNARDO SILVA

HARRY CONINX

For Callum, another future little dribbler

CONTENTS

		Page
1	Back-to-Back	7
2	Snapped Up	14
3	International Tournament	18
4	Frustration	24
5	Converting a Loan	30
6	David v Goliath	37
7	So Close, Yet So Far	44
8	Bad News	50
9	Man of the Match	58
10	A Big Goal	66
11	Champions of France	69
12	New Club, New Country	75
13	First of Many	80
14	Title	83
15	One Down, Four to Go	88
16	The Stuff of Dreams	93
17	Up for the Quadruple	98
18	Trophies	103
19	More Frustration	109
20	Within Grasp?	114
21	My Time	120

I
BACK-TO-BACK

May 2019, Amex Stadium, Brighton, England
Brighton & Hove Albion v Manchester City

The dressing room was completely silent. Bernardo glanced across the room at the players sitting opposite him – Sergio Agüero, Kevin De Bruyne and Vincent Kompany. They'd won it all, but even they looked nervous now.

"Come on, lads, let's look lively!" Pep Guardiola said, breaking the eerie silence. "We've got a game to win!"

His words made no difference. The players were on edge. Only a win today would guarantee City the title. They'd already won the League Cup, and they needed the Premier League and the FA Cup to seal a domestic treble.

"I can't believe Liverpool are still right behind us," Raheem murmured. "I was sure they'd have dropped off by now." He was sitting on the other side of the dressing room, but in the silence everybody heard what he'd said.

Pep shot him a glare. It was an unofficial rule that they weren't to mention Liverpool in the dressing room.

"Don't worry about anything else," Pep said, walking into the middle of the room. "All that matters is what we do today. We deserve to be champions, boys! The fans deserve to see champions! Get out there and win it!"

Bernardo nodded, along with the rest of the players. He felt relaxed about this game. Away at Brighton wasn't easy, but he was confident – he knew they'd win.

"Let us know what's going on in the Liverpool game," Raheem muttered to John Stones, who was on the bench for today's game.

City just needed to match Liverpool's result to seal

the title, and many of the players were keen to keep an eye on what was going on at Anfield.

The atmosphere in the Brighton stadium wasn't the most intimidating that Bernardo had experienced in England, but the importance of today's game added another level of pressure. He could feel the nerves.

City dominated the ball from the first minute, just as Pep had drilled into them over the last two seasons. But they weren't able to get their first goal.

After about 20 minutes, Bernardo glanced over at the touchline. He could see a few of the subs behind Pep whispering to each other, and then he saw John Stones mouthing the words, "one-nil".

He didn't need to be a genius to work out what that meant. Liverpool were 1-0 up.

Bernardo felt his heart sink, and suddenly his legs didn't seem to work. Were City really going to lose the title on the last day of the season? After all the hard work they'd put in, was it really going to end like this?

"Hey, Bernardo!" The shout came from Kevin De Bruyne. "Stop walking around and start putting some effort in!"

The call jolted Bernardo back into the game. There was still well over an hour to play, and he knew that City could force a goal and take the lead.

But Bernardo's belief was short-lived. A quick corner from Brighton was headed home by Glenn Murray, and suddenly City found themselves 1-0 down.

The one thing that City had feared most looked as if it was about to happen. They were about to throw the title away on the final day.

"Don't let your heads drop, boys!" Vincent Kompany roared, his voice booming around the pitch. "We've got 70 minutes to get two goals – that's all we need!"

"Let's keep playing the way we've played all year, lads!" David Silva said, clapping his hands together. "It's just another game to win!"

Just a minute later, City struck. A good ball from Laporte was flicked into the path of Sergio Agüero. The striker turned and, in typically ruthless fashion, stuck the ball into the back of the net.

City's response had been immediate and ruthless.

Bernardo sprinted over, grabbed the ball from the goal and turned back to the half-way line.

"Let's get that second and kill this game now, lads," he shouted, gesturing for them to get back for a quick restart.

Five minutes later, Bernardo had a chance to get a second goal. The cross came to him and he flung his head at it, but then watched it land comfortably in the arms of the keeper.

"I told you that you needed to practise your headers, Bernardo!" Sergio shouted. He was laughing, but Bernardo could sense that the team was frustrated that he'd missed a chance to put them ahead.

Luckily, Aymeric Laporte had been working on his headers. Just five minutes before half-time, he nodded in from a corner, and City had the second goal they'd been craving. As it stood, they were going to be Premier League champions.

"Don't give them a single chance, OK?" Pep warned the players at half-time. "We go out there, we get three or four, and we win that title."

The City players went out for the second half intent on killing any hopes Brighton had of getting back into the game.

Nearly 20 minutes into the second half, Bernardo flicked the ball into the path of Riyad Mahrez. The Algerian winger skipped past a couple of defenders and fired it into the top corner from long range.

"That's got to be enough now," Bernardo said, as the City players celebrated the goal.

They both turned to the touchline to see Pep shouting for the team to hurry up and restart the game. He wanted another goal.

"I don't think it's ever going to be enough for him," Riyad sighed, as they walked back to the centre circle.

The game was sealed with a sensational free kick from İlkay Gündoğan. The remaining minutes saw City pinging the ball from player to player, knowing that their comfortable lead would see them through.

Eventually, the ref blew his whistle for full time. With a resounding 4-1 win, City were Premier League Champions for the second year running. And, amazingly, City had won the title in both of Bernardo's seasons at the club.

"Well played, Bernardo," Vincent Kompany said. "You've had a great season – you deserve this."

The players wanted to continue the celebrations into the night. They'd sealed a second consecutive league title – and it had been hard-fought. Liverpool had pushed them all the way, and Bernardo agreed that they deserved a night off.

But Pep wasn't having it.

"We've got the FA Cup final in a couple of weeks, lads," he said. "I want to see you all in training on Monday, bright and early!"

A few players responded with groans, but Bernardo knew they would all be there. After all, Pep was a winner – and they'd all bought into his way of doing things.

In any case, Bernardo was keen to add to his trophy collection. Sealing a domestic treble seemed like the perfect way to end the season, before going off to play in the Nations League with Portugal. A few years ago, winning the title two years running and playing for his national team would have been a distant dream.

Now, it was par for the course.

And he was only just getting started.

2
SNAPPED UP

August 2003, Lisbon, Portugal

"Do you think there will be scouts, Dad?" nine-year-old Bernardo asked excitedly.

"Maybe," his dad, Mota, replied, "but we don't want to be getting ahead of ourselves."

Bernardo had met some older boys playing football in a local park in Lisbon, and they had invited him to play in a tournament out on the edge of town. Despite

Bernardo being a few years younger and quite small for his age, they'd immediately spotted how good he was. Inviting Bernardo along suited them perfectly, as they were a player short for the tournament – even though they all supported Sporting and Bernardo had already let them know he was a Benfica fan.

And it suited Bernardo too, because he'd been looking for a while for the chance to play for a proper club. There was only so long he could play in the park with all the kids his own age.

It had taken him a while to persuade his parents to let him go, but in the end they'd relented. It was the biggest tournament Bernardo had ever been in, with almost 100 teams involved. And, according to some, it was also a hotspot for scouts from all across Portugal, including some from Benfica, Porto and Sporting.

Each team at the tournament played three games on a small five-a-side pitch, and they'd play more if they won and got further in the competition. Bernardo struggled in the first game, finding himself being bullied off the ball by the bigger players.

His touch was still good and he found his team-mate

with every pass, but he wasn't quite as effective as he knew he could be.

"You're trying too much, Bernardo," his dad told him, pulling him over after the first game had ended in defeat.

"But I've got to impress the scouts," he protested. "I can't do that if I don't try anything."

"Sometimes less is more, Bernardo," Mota insisted. "You beat one man and then you pass it – you don't take on more than you can deal with."

In the next game, Bernardo got a bit more of the ball. He didn't try to do too much with it, but he did try to find his team-mates with more passes. Whenever he got the ball, he'd skip past one player, before looking to make a pass.

It was a better game for the team and they ran out comfortable winners, with Bernardo getting several assists. As the game came to a close, he turned and saw his dad giving him a thumbs-up.

Mota also nodded towards a group of men standing on the other side of the pitch.

"Scouts," he mouthed, and Bernardo turned excitedly

to see if he could work out what they were thinking. They seemed impressed but, from where he was, it was hard to read their expressions.

In the final game, Bernardo continued to follow his dad's advice. He even scored a goal, slamming the ball into the top corner after a mazy run.

"You played so well, Bernardo," Mota said, as the tournament finished. Then he pointed at one of the scouts. "This guy wants to have a word with you."

"Really?" Bernardo replied, his eyes wide.

"Yeah," his dad said, unable to hide the smile that was on his face.

The conversation was short. There was nothing the scout could say that Bernardo wouldn't agree to. It wasn't Porto or Sporting that wanted him – it was Benfica! The scout went on to explain that the finer details would be confirmed over the phone – but, by then, Bernardo had stopped listening.

He was going to play for the club he'd supported since he was a baby.

He was going to be a professional footballer.

3
INTERNATIONAL TOURNAMENT

July 2013, Alytus Stadium, Alytus, Lithuania
U19 European Championships Semi-Final, Serbia v Portugal

"It's just frustrating," Bernardo complained to João Cancelo during a gym session.

"The manager's just easing you in," João replied. "Too many players are rushed into the team early – and then they never make it."

It had been over ten years now since Bernardo had been picked up by Benfica. In that time, he'd made his way through the ranks and had played for every Benfica youth team. But he was yet to make his debut.

He was still only 18, but at his age a lot of the top players had already played full seasons. Yet he was still stuck in the Portuguese Juniors Championship – not even the Benfica B team.

Bernardo knew that João was trying to make him feel better, but he wasn't persuaded. Bernardo's plans to make it as a footballer did not include sitting in the reserve team until he was in his twenties.

At Benfica, the rest of the players referred to Bernardo as "Little Messi". It was intended as a compliment, but, as Bernardo was always keen to point out, he was actually an inch taller than Messi. And Messi – like Ronaldo – had made his debut at the age of 17.

But Bernardo was already building a reputation online, and videos of his performances and highlights had been shared all around Portugal. Pressure was building on the Benfica manager, Jorge Jesus, to include him in the first team.

Despite not making his debut, he was learning a lot at Benfica about tactics and technique.

He was constantly being told when to hold his position on the left-hand side, and when was a good time to track back and help defend. But the coaches didn't want him to lose the natural ability that he'd developed, playing in the parks across Lisbon.

"You need to improve your shooting, Bernardo," João Tralhão, Benfica's youth team manager, told him.

"My dad always said it's better to be a good passer and dribbler than to be able to shoot well," Bernardo replied. His dad had always told him that he'd be appreciated more if he could pass. Nobody liked the guy who had 30 shots – even if he scored with 10 of them.

"Normally I'd agree with you, Bernardo," Tralhão replied. "Most kids need to be taught *not* to shoot – but you're different to most of them. "When I watch you, there's so many times I'm thinking, 'SHOOT, just shoot!' – and then I look up, and you've tried to nutmeg another player, or pass it back to someone else."

"But what if I don't score?" Bernardo objected. "Surely I should try and pass it to someone who might be better at shooting than me?"

"Well, then you need to make sure that there aren't

many people who *are* better than you. Which means – work on your shooting."

"What should I do in the actual games?" Bernardo asked. "Do you have any tips for me?"

"I think for the time being, just aim for the bottom corners – it's much harder for the keepers to get down there. And my only other piece of advice is to really put your foot through it. I know it sounds obvious, but some players try to pass it into the corner of the goal. Your best bet is to just smash it."

Bernardo quickly started following Tralhão's advice in matches, adding a few goals to his game. It made him feel more confident too. When Benfica Youth won the Portuguese Juniors Championship in 2013, Bernardo was at the centre of it.

But none of it seemed to impress Jorge Jesus.

However, Bernardo had impressed the Portugal U19 manager, Emílio Peixe, and he was selected for the U19 European Championships that very summer, alongside a number of his Benfica team-mates, including João Cancelo.

The tournament was being held in Lithuania, and

the whole squad was staying together in a hotel, just as the main squad would do.

"It's like we're playing in the actual Euros!" João Cancelo babbled excitedly, as they checked in at the hotel.

Portugal had one of the better squads at the tournament and, together with France and Spain, were amongst the favourites to win it.

The opening match, against their old rivals, Spain, was one of the toughest games of the tournament, and Spain proved the better side, deservedly winning 1-0.

The next two games were against the Netherlands and the hosts, Lithuania. Portugal scored four in each, with Bernardo heavily involved.

"I wonder if Jesus is watching," João Cancelo asked.

"I doubt it," Bernardo grumbled. "And even if he is, he probably still wouldn't pick us."

Portugal were up against Serbia in the semi-final, and the players knew that it was going to be a tough game. Serbia took the lead early and it looked as if Portugal's journey was coming to an end.

Bernardo got the ball on the right-hand side, playing

a quick one-two with Ricardo Horta, before entering the box. The ball came back to him and, whilst it was in the air, Bernardo volleyed it hard and low into the far corner.

Finally, he had his goal. He had levelled the scores.

"I told you, man, didn't I?" João Cancelo roared, as the team chased him in celebration.

Portugal took the lead through Alex Guedes, but a late Serbia equaliser sent the game to a penalty shootout.

Bernardo was on the bench by this stage, exhausted after four consecutive games, and he could only watch in complete frustration as Portugal missed three of their five penalties and were dumped out.

It was devastating to have got so close to a potential trophy, only to stumble at the last hurdle.

There was some consolation for Bernardo, as he had been named by UEFA as one of the top 10 talents under the age of 19 across the whole of Europe.

Surely, there was no way that Jorge Jesus could ignore him now.

4
FRUSTRATION

October 2013, Estádio Municipal Cerveira Pinto,
Cinfães, Portugal, CD Cinfães v S.L. Benfica

"I saw you at the Euros, Bernardo. Between you and me, I'm surprised the boss has put you with us, and not brought you into the first team," the Benfica B-team manager, Hélder Cristóvão, told him.

Bernardo wasn't happy about being excluded from the first team, but they were flying high without him, so Jesus was clearly doing something right.

It was a bittersweet feeling. Bernardo loved seeing his team doing well but, on the other hand, he knew that his chances of getting into the team were disappearing.

"If you keep your head down, I wouldn't be surprised if Jorge calls you up before January," Cristóvão added.

Bernardo was pleased to hear that. Hélder had seen a lot of top players come through the Benfica academy and, if he thought that Bernardo was as good as any of those guys, then it was a huge compliment.

Hélder Cristóvão was very happy to have Bernardo in his B-team, and the new manager had already made it clear that he was a big part of his plans.

Bernardo got his first start against Braga B, and was heavily involved in all three of the goals Benfica scored. That included Bernardo's first goal, a powerful finish that flew past the keeper.

He had formed a good partnership down the right-hand side with João Cancelo, and both of them were attracting attention. Bernardo even won the Segunda Division Player of the Month for October.

Eventually, the moment he'd been waiting for

arrived, when he was called up for the Benfica first team.

It wasn't the glamorous debut he'd pictured as a kid, starting in front of 60,000 roaring fans at the Estádio da Luz. Rather, it was a cup game at CD Cinfães, and he was on the bench.

But still, there was a good chance he'd get on the pitch and make his debut.

Cancelo started on the bench too, alongside Bernardo. Ola John put Benfica ahead in the second half but, with only 15 minutes of the match remaining, there was no sign of either Bernardo or João going on.

Then, on the 80th minute mark, Jesus turned to Bernardo.

"Go on, get out there, son," Jesus said. "We've got a narrow lead, so let's just try and hold onto it. You need to work hard defensively."

Bernardo's ten minutes on the pitch were slow. He struggled to get the ball, and there were no opportunities for him to show his brilliance. Every time he pushed forward, he got a glare from Jesus.

It was nothing like he'd imagined his debut would

be. He'd pictured being the star of the show, scoring a hat-trick to beat Porto 3-0.

"You're annoyed, aren't you?" Cancelo said, as Bernardo stomped off the pitch at the end of the game.

"I barely touched it," Bernardo protested. "How am I supposed to get into the first team, if the boss won't let me get past the half-way line?"

Hélder Cristóvão was sympathetic to his protests.

"You've got to keep working, Bernardo," he said. "Trust me, it will come."

"I don't think Jesus likes me," Bernardo sighed. "I don't think there's anything I can do about it."

Hélder offered to speak to Jesus, and afterwards he spoke to Bernardo again.

"I spoke to Jorge, and I think the issue is that he's not sure you can do as much for the team going forward," Hélder said. "He wanted to know if you'd be interested in retraining as a full-back, or trying to become a bit more defensively-minded."

"What?" Bernardo said, completely shocked. "How can he say that? I'm an attacking midfielder – that's what I've always been!"

"I know. I tried, Bernardo. I'm sorry – I don't know if it's going to work out."

Bernardo felt completely crushed.

Benfica had felt like his destiny since he'd been a little kid, but now it looked as though he might have to find a new club.

The Benfica first team continued to win game after game and looked set for a clean sweep of trophies. Their final game of the season was away at Porto, but by then the title was already won.

So, with the Europa League final coming up, Jesus had picked a squad of young players – including Bernardo – for the game.

Bernardo was left on the bench, but this time he wasn't particularly upset. He'd already decided to push for some kind of transfer in the summer.

He did eventually come on for the last ten minutes, but again he struggled to get involved in the game. It was ultimately a 2-1 defeat, but nobody in the stadium particularly cared, least of all Bernardo.

He even got himself medals for the two cups wins and the league title, but he didn't really know what to do with them. He hadn't earned them – he didn't deserve them.

It didn't matter. Nothing mattered.

He was going to leave Benfica this year.

5
CONVERTING A LOAN

January 2015, AS Monaco FC Training Centre,
La Turbie, France

"I don't want to lose you, Bernardo, but if you're not prepared to put the effort in to stay here, then I can understand why you're leaving," Jorge Jesus said.

Bernardo didn't reply. He saw no point in arguing – he was just happy to get out of there, even though it was hard for him to leave his boyhood team.

The one thing Bernardo did insist on was a loan

move. If a new manager came in at Benfica, Bernardo wanted to be able to come back. A part of him still hoped that he could succeed at Benfica.

Bernardo had a number of loan offers to consider, but the one that caught his eye was from Monaco, in France. The squad had a reputation for developing young players, and included the likes of Anthony Martial and Fabinho. They also had another Portuguese player, in João Moutinho. Moutinho was a legend in Portugal, and the opportunity to play alongside him was one that Bernardo couldn't pass up.

The team was managed by Leonardo Jardim and, from the very first meeting, Bernardo knew that he was going to get on better with this man than with Jorge Jesus.

"You're going to be a star man for us, OK, Bernardo?" Jardim told him. "I'm planning to use you as our main attacking midfielder, supporting Berba and Carrasco. I want to ease you in, so you might not start the first few games, but I don't want you to think that I'm not being straight with you. You're going to be a key part of our team this season."

Jardim was true to his word and, at the beginning, Bernardo spent a lot of time on the bench.

Slowly he got used to Monaco's style of play. They preferred to use quick passes and clever through-balls, and there wasn't such reliance on being big or strong, which he'd heard that French football was famous for.

"I thought it was all muddy slide-tackles and big crosses here," Bernardo said to Moutinho, after one training session. They'd spent the whole session keeping the ball on the ground, with the manager insisting that they didn't play it in the air.

"Not here at Monaco," Moutinho laughed. "And actually, not really in France at all – not any more."

"I could get used to this," Bernardo grinned.

Monaco had a reputation for being one of the best teams in France, but in recent years they'd lost their way. PSG were now the dominant team, and it was going to be a huge challenge to overtake them.

Jardim had decided that Monaco would do just that – and Bernardo was to be a key player in the team he was putting together.

Bernardo's first start came in late September, playing

as part of an attacking three behind Dimitar Berbatov in a game against Guingamp.

"Just play your normal game out there, Bernardo," Jardim told him before the game. "Lots of dribbling, lots of running. Dimi hasn't got a lot of running in him any more, so you guys are going to have to cover for him."

This is what they'd been practising in training, and Bernardo was ready for this role.

The game got off to a poor start, when Anthony Martial limped off after just 23 minutes. But it actually worked out well for Monaco, as his replacement, Nabil Dirar, scored the first and only goal for them, giving them a crucial win.

Bernardo came off the pitch feeling disappointed. He thought he'd been pretty much non-existent throughout.

"You were brilliant out there!" Jardim told him. "We couldn't have won this game without you."

"Thanks," Bernardo replied. "I'm sorry I didn't score or anything."

"What? That doesn't matter," Jardim laughed. "You did all I asked you to do – and more!"

As the season went on, Bernardo began to play

more games, sometimes playing the full 90 minutes, sometimes coming off the bench. But, unlike the situation at Benfica, here he had faith in his manager. He knew that there was a plan for him.

Monaco were in decent form, in both the league and the Champions League. They were engaged with a number of teams, including rivals Marseille, in a tough battle for the top four.

And it was Marseille that they faced next.

Bernardo started the game, alongside Carrasco, Martial and Nabil Dirar. There was no Berbatov up front today, so Bernardo's role was a little different.

"You don't need to do so much running today, alright Bernardo?" Jardim said. "Anthony is quick, so see if you can play passes in behind, put their defence on the back foot."

Bernardo appreciated the detailed instructions that he always got from Jardim before a match. He was being told which approach to take in each game – and he was learning for himself how to spot the best approach to take.

There were few chances in a tight first half, and

it wasn't until the second half that the deadlock was broken.

Martial burst down the right-hand side, whipping a ball into the box. Bernardo had burst from deep and was waiting in the box. He took one touch and smashed it into the bottom corner, low and hard, just as he'd been taught by João Tralhão all those years ago.

The Monaco fans were bouncing.

"Come on!" Bernardo roared, celebrating the goal in front of the fans. It was a huge goal for the club and their top-four ambitions.

"That's your first Monaco goal, right, Bernardo?" Moutinho said, clapping him on the back.

"Yeah! How could you not have realised?" Bernardo joked.

"And what a time to get it!" Carrasco shouted, still giddy from the opener.

Monaco held on for the 1-0 win – a big win in Monaco's pursuit of European football, and a big moment in Bernardo's career.

He didn't see Monaco as a loan move any more – he wanted to stay with the club permanently.

In January, the good news was broken to him. Monaco had made a bid of around 15 million for him, to change his loan move into a permanent one. Jorge Jesus hadn't thought twice about letting him go, and Bernardo hadn't needed any convincing.

Before January was over, he'd put pen to paper.

Still just 20 years old, Bernardo hadn't anticipated leaving Benfica this early in his career.

But, right now, he couldn't imagine himself playing for anyone other than Leonardo Jardim.

6
DAVID V GOLIATH

February 2015, Emirates Stadium, London, England
UEFA Champions League, Arsenal v AS Monaco

"Remember, we're going as opponents, not fans," Nabil Dirar warned, as he caught Bernardo scrolling through Arsenal's Twitter feed.

"I know, I know," Bernardo said. Although he was a fan of Arsenal – and of the Premier League – that didn't mean that he couldn't compete with them and challenge them.

Despite Bernardo's form, Monaco were a long way adrift of runaway leaders PSG in the title race. There had never been any real hope that they could compete with PSG's financial muscle, but Monaco were still in the Champions League and the Coupe de France. They could still end the season with silverware.

Monaco had topped their Champions League group without much trouble, but in the last-16 they had their toughest challenge – Arsenal.

The Arsenal team was packed with star names, including Santi Cazorla, Mesut Özil and Alexis Sánchez. Özil was one player that Bernardo was particularly excited to see.

Bernardo's motivation was tested when he saw the Emirates Stadium. He'd played in big stadiums before – in Portugal and in France, but even he was a little taken aback by the size of the Emirates.

"Look at the grass!" Fabinho whispered. Bernardo had never seen grass like it. It was in such pristine condition, it almost felt like a crime to play on it.

"Imagine how slick our passing is going to be," Fabinho continued. "We'll slice them open easily."

"Or they'll do it to us," João Moutinho said, overhearing the conversation. "They play half their games on this pitch, remember. This isn't going to be easy."

Bernardo felt the familiar build-up of nerves as they settled into the dressing room. This was arguably the biggest game of Monaco's season so far – and it was certainly the biggest of his career so far.

Jardim waited until the last moment to announce the starting line-up, and Bernardo sat in the dressing room, waiting for his name to be called.

But the manager didn't call him.

Bernardo tried not to show it, but he felt a huge sense of disappointment – and a little bit of anger. He'd been in fine form, but now, in the biggest game of the season, he'd been dropped.

Leonardo Jardim caught up with him as they headed out of the dressing room to the tunnel.

"Sorry about this, Bernardo," he said, a little hesitantly.

"It's fine," Bernardo replied, not making eye contact.

"You're not being dropped," Jardim continued. "It's

just about the opposition. Arsenal are going to dominate the ball – we're not going to have a lot of it, right?"

He paused, making sure that Bernardo was listening. "So we're going to try and hit them on the counter-attack, with quick players like Martial and Dirar."

Bernardo nodded. He still didn't see why he couldn't have played in a more central role. But Jardim was one step ahead of him.

"I also need the midfield to be a bit more defensively minded – and a bit more experienced," he said. "We'll get you on though, I promise."

Leonardo Jardim was absolutely right about the match. Arsenal were dominant, and Monaco couldn't get the ball off them at all. It seemed to everyone on the Monaco bench that they were heading for a heavy defeat.

Not long before half-time, the ball came to Geoffrey Kondogbia at the edge of the box. His first touch set the ball nicely ahead of him, and with his second he fired it past Ospina into the Arsenal goal.

Monaco were one-up against Arsenal.

"Come on!" Bernardo grunted, punching the air with his fist.

"That away goal will be crucial," Carrasco muttered next to him.

The second half continued in a similar manner. Arsenal were dominant in possession, but every time Monaco came forward they looked as if they might score.

"There's so much space out there," Carrasco said, excited at the thought that he might get on.

Olivier Giroud missed several early chances in the second half and, each time, he thumped the ground in frustration.

Ten minutes into the second half, Monaco broke once more. Anthony Martial got away from the Arsenal defence and fed Dimitar Berbatov. The Bulgarian striker was ice-cold in front of goal and slammed it into the top corner.

Now Monaco were 2-0 up – away, at Arsenal!

"Make sure we concentrate now, boys," Bernardo heard Jardim shout from the touchline, clearly bracing himself for an Arsenal onslaught.

Monaco continued to stand firm, and Arsenal continued to miss easy chances. With six minutes to go, Jardim beckoned Bernardo forward.

"Get out there and just try and hold on to the ball, get it as far away from our goal as you can," he said, breathlessly. The manager had been doing as much running up and down the touchline as some of the players.

For five minutes, Bernardo barely touched the ball. It was all defending and positioning – parts of his game that he hadn't spent a lot of time on.

As the clock ticked over the 90th minute, Alex Oxlade-Chamberlain got the ball on the edge of the Monaco box. He flicked it past one defender, before curling a sensational effort into the top corner.

It was 2-1.

"Let's not lose this now, lads," Moutinho bellowed, trying to raise the Monaco players' spirits. A 2-1 win away from home was still a good result – even a 2-2 draw would be good. But Monaco wanted the win.

A couple of minutes later, Bernardo picked the ball up on the half-way line, dancing away with it from an

Arsenal defender. In the corner of his eye he spotted Yannick Carrasco bursting through, sprinting at full pelt.

"Bernardo!" Carrasco roared. "Now!"

With expert precision, Bernardo played the ball behind an Arsenal defender and into the feet of the onrushing Carrasco. His first touch was excellent, taking him away from the chasing Arsenal defence. He burst into the box and fired the ball past Ospina.

That was 3-1. Game over.

"I'm glad we made the most of that space," Bernardo joked with Carrasco as they celebrated.

The home crowd had been stunned into silence by the French side's ruthless finishing. Even if Monaco didn't score in the second leg, Arsenal would have to score three goals to overturn the deficit, because of away goals.

As they left the pitch, Jardim hugged Monaco's newest wonderkid.

"Told you you'd get on, didn't I?"

7
SO CLOSE, YET SO FAR

June 2015, Eden Aréna, Prague, Czech Republic
U21 European Championships

The miracle comeback almost happened, as Arsenal won 2-0 at Monaco in the second leg. But it wasn't enough, and Monaco went through on away goals – only to be dumped out of the competition by Juventus in the quarter-finals.

Bernardo, however, did achieve one of his own personal goals, making his international debut for

Portugal, in March. It was only in a friendly, and it was only against Cape Verde but, even so, it was one of the best moments of his life.

The Portugal manager, Fernando Santos, had been keen to experiment, and he had picked a number of youngsters and less-experienced players for the game. None of the big guns were playing this time, and the result was disappointing, as Portugal lost 2-0 to minnows Cape Verde.

"You were a little stiff out there, Bernardo," Santos said, speaking to him after the game. "Were you nervous?"

"Maybe a little bit," Bernardo admitted, knowing full-well that he'd been totally terrified out there.

"Well, try not to be," Santos continued, giving him a comforting smile. "I've watched you play for Monaco – you belong in this squad."

Even if the game itself had been a disappointment, Bernardo had been inspired by his appearance for his country. He was an international footballer now.

Bernardo returned to Monaco in the best form of his life, and he finished the season with 10 goals. Only

Martial had scored more for Monaco this season. Monaco finished third in the league, securing their place in the Champions League for another year, at least.

That wasn't the end of the season for Bernardo, though, as he was playing for the Portugal U21s in the U21 Euros. It was a good opportunity for him to test himself, as well as to catch up with some of his old friends from Benfica who would be in the squad.

The first game was against the pre-tournament favourites, England. It was a tight game and England had a number of strong players, including Harry Kane and Jesse Lingard.

As it turned out, the game was decided with only a single goal. An effort from Bernardo was saved, and João Mário crashed home the rebound, giving Portugal the victory.

"If we can beat England, we can beat anyone," Bernardo told João Cancelo. "You know, we might actually win this!"

They ended up drawing their next two games, against Italy and Sweden, but it was enough to send Portugal through to the semi-finals.

If England had been a tough game, this was likely to be even harder. It was against Germany. Would this be the end of Portugal's run in the competition?

They got off to the perfect start. After 25 minutes, Bernardo got the ball on the left-hand side of the box. He opened up his body and fired it over the keeper and into the back of the net.

GOAL!

He sprinted to the corner flag, where he was quickly joined by his team-mates in celebration.

"Let's go and get a second now, lads," he said, pumped up by the joy of scoring a goal.

Ricardo Pereira added a second from a corner about 10 minutes later, and then, just before half-time, Ivan Cavaleiro smashed Portugal into a 3-0 lead.

"What is happening?" Bernardo shouted, in disbelief. They weren't just beating Germany – they were thrashing them. What had they been so worried about?

Portugal added two more in the second half, thanks to João Mário and Ricardo Horta. They had beaten Germany 5-0 – and now the only team standing in their way was Sweden.

"Lads, if we play like that again, we can beat anyone," William Carvalho told the players, as they gathered in a huddle after the Germany match. "It doesn't matter if it's Sweden U21 or their first team – if we play like that, we will win."

Portugal and Sweden had played out a tight draw in the group stage, and the final followed the same pattern. For 120 minutes, both teams tested each other, attempting to lure their opponent, but with nobody quite willing to commit to an attack.

At the final whistle, the score was still 0-0. It was going to a penalty shootout.

Bernardo was exhausted. He was desperate to take a penalty, to help his team win, but his body told him otherwise – and he was wise enough to listen.

"I can't do it, boss," he wheezed, almost collapsing on the floor as he spoke to the manager. "I can't be in the first five. Put me further down the list."

The first five penalties were all scored, and it looked as if it was going to be a long shootout. Bernardo might be called into action after all.

But it wasn't to be. Portugal's talisman, and their best

player at this tournament, William Carvalho, missed his crucial spot kick, as the Swedish keeper pushed it away to win the competition for them.

Sweden were crowned champions and, just as in the U19 Euros, it was a story of "so close yet so far" for Bernardo.

Bernardo was crushed, but he'd loved the tournament. He was desperate to be involved in the main one next summer. He vowed that if it went to penalties again, he'd be up there taking one.

He wasn't going to let his country and his team down again.

8
BAD NEWS

August 2015,

AS Monaco FC Training Center, La Turbie, France

"Is anyone staying here?" Bernardo asked Fabinho desperately during one training session, after they'd just found out that Geoffrey Kondogbia was joining Inter Milan.

"Well, I've just signed permanently," Fabinho replied. "No more loan for me."

"That doesn't count!" Bernardo protested. "But

still, we're only going to have me and you if we're not careful."

"I'm sure the boss has got a plan or two up his sleeve," Fabinho replied.

Bernardo knew that the summer would be full of changes at Monaco, a club that many players saw as a stepping-stone to bigger clubs. Layvin Kurzawa had departed to rivals PSG, Berbatov had gone to PAOK in Greece, and Carrasco had signed for Atlético Madrid.

Thomas Lemar, one of the biggest young talents in France, was one of the only permanent signings arriving at Monaco. The others were all loans, and Bernardo was worried that Monaco might slip back, after all the good progress they'd made over the previous season.

"How come we can't get anyone permanently?" he murmured to João Moutinho. He was overheard by Ricardo Carvalho, who was sitting on a table behind them.

"Spending a lot of money doesn't always mean you're getting quality," Ricardo warned. He had experience at big clubs like Chelsea and Real Madrid.

"Loads of our big-money signings at Madrid turned

out to be dreadful, but some of the loan signings ended up being better than expected."

He was right, and Monaco's loan signings included some quality players. Mario Pašalic´ arrived from Chelsea, Stephane El Shaarawy joined from AC Milan, and the best one in Bernardo's mind was the arrival of fellow Portuguese Fábio Coentrão, from Real Madrid.

Now it was time to focus on the team's important upcoming matches.

After sneaking into the top four in the league, Monaco had qualifying games to get through, before the Champions League group stages.

They thrashed Swiss team Young Boys, setting up a tie against Valencia.

The Spaniards proved to be too quick, too strong and too good and, with Monaco 3-1 down after the first leg, they were unable to turn the tie around.

Monaco were demoted to the Europa League, but things then went from bad to worse when they started to struggle in the league as well. They were conceding as many goals as they scored, and they'd been soundly beaten by PSG.

Bernardo was out of form too, which made matters worse. He'd scored in the opening league match of the season against Nice, but he'd felt a little sluggish. His passes weren't accurate and his touch was loose.

"How can we be out of the title race after barely five games?" Bernardo moaned once more to Fabinho, who was getting rather used to Bernardo's continual complaints.

"We're not," Fabinho laughed. "Anyway, there's so many new players around here, we're still all getting used to each other, working out how everyone plays. We just need a bit of time."

It was true. Bernardo hadn't had a lot of conversations with Mario Pašalic´ or Ivan Cavaleiro. If he wanted the team to flow better, perhaps he needed to talk with them, understand how they worked.

Ivan Cavaleiro was part of a large group of Portuguese players currently at the club. They were almost starting to form a team within a team, with their own little methods of play.

Monaco's form was picking up in the league, but Bernardo wasn't getting anywhere near the number of goals or assists he wanted. He set himself targets every year for what he wanted to achieve. He'd scored ten goals last season, and he'd been keen to at least match that this year, but he was already way off.

"You look frustrated, Bernardo," Leonardo Jardim said, putting an arm around him after a long training session. It was bitterly cold and Bernardo was exhausted.

"I should be doing better this season, boss," he said, finally laying out his concerns to the manager. "I've barely scored – or even assisted."

"Personally, I want the whole team to be doing better," Jardim said. "Of course I do – but I don't think you've been performing badly at all. It's not all about goals and assists, Bernardo. Football isn't all about statistics. You've been playing really well, and I know it's been difficult for you. We've had a lot of new faces to try and get into the team."

"I guess," Bernardo replied, a little hesitantly. This was a very different situation to any he'd experienced back in his time at Benfica. It felt a little odd having the full support of the manager, even when he felt he wasn't playing well.

The January transfer window brought a few more changes at Monaco. El Shaarawy departed, as his loan ended and he returned to AC Milan, and Vágner Love came in from Corinthians, to boost Monaco's striking options.

January also brought an upturn in form. They were out of the cups, but they were winning games in the league. They were now up to second place, although they were still a long way adrift of PSG.

Bernardo wouldn't admit it to anyone at the club, but his main focus was no longer Monaco. He had his eye on a bigger goal. The 2016 European Championships were coming up, and he was desperate to be part of Portugal's squad. He'd even got word – unofficially – that he was going to be in the squad.

The next game for Monaco was away at Lyon.

Monaco had slipped down to third, but they were still pretty much assured of Champions League football next season, and this game was little more than a friendly.

The game started poorly, with Lyon scoring twice within the first 10 minutes. After 23 minutes it went from bad to worse, as striker Lacina Traoré was sent off.

"I know we're down to 10 men, but we can still get a result here!" Bernardo shouted to the players, trying to turn things around.

It continued to go downhill. Lyon scored twice more, and at half-time they were well clear, despite Ricardo Carvalho pulling a goal back.

In the second half, Lyon quickly made it 5-1, and the Monaco players could see that there was no way back. They were being absolutely thrashed.

Then, as Bernardo chased a loose ball, he suddenly felt pain in the back of his thigh. It tightened up quickly and he eventually limped to a halt and slumped to the floor.

He turned and signalled to the bench. He couldn't go on – his match was over.

As he hobbled down the tunnel, supported by a physio, only one thought crossed his mind.

The Euros. Would he be fit?

It was a tense wait for the results – and the news was bad. He would be out for another six weeks.

Bernardo got the call from the Portugal manager a week later.

"The Monaco doctor told me you might recover in time for the quarter-finals, Bernardo," Santos told him. "But I need a squad that's going to be fit for the whole tournament. I'm really sorry, but I'm going to have to leave you out, Bernardo."

The news was devastating, even though Bernardo had been expecting the decision. Now he'd be watching the tournament on TV.

But even that became painful, when Portugal went all the way to the final and lifted the trophy.

"I'm happy for them, but I know I would have been there if I wasn't injured," Bernardo said to his dad.

"You're still so young, son. You can't control everything. You'll have the chance to win the Euros another time," his dad replied. "Anyway, shouldn't you be thinking about winning trophies at Monaco now?"

9
MAN OF THE MATCH

January 2017, Stade Velodrome, Marseille, France
Olympique de Marseille v AS Monaco

"It was incredible, mate. It's a shame you weren't there."

When Bernardo had first joined Monaco, having João Moutinho as a team-mate had been the best thing in the world. But now it felt like the worst. Bernardo had to listen to João telling constant stories about the European Championships win – and with every story, Bernardo felt the pain that he'd not been there.

Most of the other Portuguese players had left during another summer of change at Monaco, with some new players coming in, including Radamel Falcao and Djibril Sidibé.

"I think we can really push PSG all the way this year," Bernardo said, after a tough training session, interrupting another of Moutinho's tales from the Euros.

"Push them all the way?" Falcao said, overhearing their conversation. "We want to win this thing."

Bernardo had played with Cristiano Ronaldo in the Portugal squad, so it was rare that he was intimidated by any players. But Falcao had an air of confidence about him that was inspiring to the rest of the side. He'd had some bad years with Chelsea and Man United, but his positive attitude this season was uplifting.

The first challenge for Monaco was getting through the Champions League qualifiers – something they'd failed to do last year. They started in good form, first knocking out Fenerbahçe, before beating Spanish giants Villarreal.

Bernardo had actually scored against Villarreal, fizzing a left-footed shot past the keeper. It was already his second goal of the season, after he'd scored on the opening day against Guingamp. Despite Jardim's reassurances last season, Bernardo was desperate to add more goals to his game.

Although Bernardo's summer had been desperately disappointing, missing out on the Euros through injury, there had been one bright spot. Leonardo Jardim had handed him the number 10 shirt at Monaco.

"Why me?" he'd asked, sure there were other players who might have deserved it more.

"You're my main man, Bernardo," Jardim had replied. "You're our little Messi – and I need you to start believing that. If wearing the number 10 helps, then I'll put the shirt on you myself before every game."

Monaco started the league season strongly, winning four of their opening five games, including a 3-1 thrashing of PSG at the Stade Louis II.

The stadium wasn't the biggest, but the roar after the final whistle was deafening. At full time, Bernardo went over to an exhausted Bakayoko and Fabinho. It was rare for anyone to beat PSG, so the Monaco players had to savour nights like these.

"He might be right, you know," Bernardo said. "We really might win this thing."

"It's not even September yet, Bernardo," Fabinho said, laughing and pushing him away. "Let's chill out a bit."

The next few months were inconsistent for Monaco. They were scoring more goals than ever, but they were struggling at the other end. Young superstar Kylian Mbappé was now part of the squad, and Jardim was trying to balance him, Falcao, Valère Germain, Thomas Lemar and Bernardo into a front three.

"We're going to have to do it," Jardim sighed after one game, looking at his tactical whiteboard. He nudged one of the pieces into a different position. "We're going to have to go to a 4-4-2."

The new 4-4-2 setup changed everything for Monaco. Now they had two playmakers on the wings, in Bernardo and Thomas Lemar, who would drift into the centre of the pitch. This left lots of space outside them for their attacking full-backs to overlap. In the middle, they had pace in Mbappé and clinical finishing and experience in Falcao.

It meant that Bakayoko and Fabinho had plenty of work to do in the middle, but Monaco now lived by a simple philosophy. However many goals the opposition scored, they were going to score more.

The new setup quickly showed in their results. They would often get big results, where they were absolutely dominant, but this would be followed by a heavy defeat. A 4-1 win away at Lille was followed a couple of weeks later by a 4-0 defeat to Nice. A 7-0 win at Metz was followed by a 3-1 defeat to Toulouse.

They still couldn't find consistency.

Bernardo was thriving in the system, though. He'd scored his first goal for Portugal in September, although he hadn't scored in the league since the start of the season. But he was in the best form of his life and he wasn't worried.

"None of them can get near you, Bernardo," Moutinho remarked, after one game.

"I wish I could get a bit closer to the goal though," Bernardo moaned. "I might be able to get a shot away then, grab a goal."

"That's not your job," João said. "You exhaust the

defenders, turn them inside-out – and if you can get the ball into Falcao and Kylian, they'll finish it off."

He was right. Bernardo and Thomas Lemar were the creators – they weren't there to finish off chances, but to create them.

The ups and downs they'd had in the league hadn't troubled them in the Champions League. They'd beaten Tottenham both home and away, and had thrashed CSKA Moscow, to ensure their place in the knockout stages.

Monaco's form in the league gradually improved and, despite a 3-1 defeat to Montpellier, they were now just a couple of points behind PSG.

Their next game in the league was away at Marseille.

"We win this game, boys, and we go top of the league!" Falcao told the players before the game.

"If we go top – then we make sure we keep it for the rest of the season," Fabinho added confidently.

The game got off to the perfect start. Fifteen minutes in, Thomas Lemar looped the ball over the Marseille keeper to put the visitors one-up.

Five minutes later, the advantage was doubled.

Bakayoko slipped in Falcao, who dinked it over the goalkeeper and into the back of the net.

"Come on!" he roared, and even from over 40 yards away, Bernardo heard the shout. The team wanted this.

About 10 minutes later, a Rolando header pulled one back for Marseille.

"Keep it tight, lads!" Jardim shouted from the touchline, although he knew that he was wasting his breath. Keeping it tight wasn't how Monaco played.

A few seconds before half-time, Bernardo picked the ball up and drove towards the goal, before slipping the ball out wide.

"Cross it!" he roared, sprinting into the middle of the box.

The ball flew through the air and Bernardo met it with his head, powering it past the despairing Marseille keeper.

GOAL!

He ran off with Falcao, celebrating his league goal.

"Bet you're proud of that one, mate! Who'd have thought the smallest guy on the pitch would score a header?" the captain said.

Then, 10 minutes into the second half, Bernardo had another. Fabinho burst into the box, but his effort was saved. The ball rebounded to Bernardo, who whipped it into the top of the goal.

Bernardo had gone 11 games without a league goal. Now he had two in a single match, and the Man of the Match award to go with it.

The final whistle went and Monaco were top of the league. They'd only lost once in their last 11 games.

"No one can stop us now!" Falcao shouted, as the players danced in the changing room after the match.

But Bernardo could see that Jardim wanted to calm the players.

The Man of the Match raised his voice.

"One game at a time, boys! One game at a time."

10
A BIG GOAL

January 2017, Parc des Princes, Paris, France
Paris Saint-Germain v AS Monaco

Not long after the Marseille game, Monaco were preparing for their biggest test of the season – PSG. The Parisians were still riding high, but they had slipped to third in the table, a point behind Nice.

This was a match that neither team could afford to lose.

"We win this and we knock PSG out of the title race,

lads!" Fabinho shouted, silencing any conversations in the dressing room.

He was right. A win would put Monaco six points clear of PSG and, with the form they were in, it would be a huge ask for PSG to catch them.

But it wasn't going to be easy. The PSG team was brimming with superstars, including Edinson Cavani and Thiago Silva.

The game was played at a fast pace in pouring rain, with the ball skidding and sliding all over the place.

"Don't be afraid to have a shot!" Falcao roared, over the cheers of the fans. "The ball will skid – it might throw off the keeper!"

As expected, the match was a cagey affair, and with ten minutes to go it was still 0-0. It was unlike Monaco to get so far into a game without scoring.

A cross came into the Monaco box and Julian Draxler flung himself at the ball, but then suddenly fell to the floor.

"PENALTY!" the fans and players shouted in unison. The referee decided that Draxler had been pushed by Sidibé, and pointed to the spot.

Bernardo kicked the air in frustration. He couldn't believe that they were going to lose this game at the last moment.

Cavani stepped up to take the penalty – and calmly put it away, sending the keeper the wrong way.

The pressure was now on Monaco. They had 10 minutes to snatch something from this game.

Each minute seemed to go past in a few seconds, as the 90th minute came and went.

Bernardo got the ball on the right-hand side and cut inside, pushing towards the box. He remembered Falcao's advice from earlier, about trying it on with a shot, so he fired the ball towards goal.

It skidded across the wet turf and sailed past the keeper.

GOAL!

Bernardo sprinted towards the corner flag.

"YESSSSSS!" came the shout from the Monaco players behind him, as they piled together in a huge huddle.

That equaliser could be the goal that won them the title. And it was Bernardo who'd scored it.

11
CHAMPIONS OF FRANCE

May 2017, Stade Louis II, Monte Carlo, Monaco
Monaco v St-Étienne

"Kylian is the key," Jardim told Bernardo in a team meeting, a few days before the first leg. "They won't know how to handle his pace, so see if you can get the ball in behind to him."

The wins continued to flow in the league – and so did the goals. Monaco were top on goal difference, and they weren't letting that go.

The Champions League last-16 had set them up with a tie against English giants Man City, coached by the legendary Pep Guardiola.

The first tie was away at the Etihad Stadium and, despite City's immense quality, Monaco weren't going to change their approach. Jardim stuck with 4-4-2, putting the young Kylian Mbappé up front.

The first leg was end-to-end, just the way Monaco liked it. City took an early lead, but Monaco struck back twice before half-time, through Falcao and Mbappé, to go in 2-1 up.

In the second half, Monaco continued to push forward, but defensively they weren't able to match City's quality, and the game ended in a 5-3 defeat.

It was a disappointment for Monaco, but they knew that three away goals gave them a good chance of making the next round.

As Bernardo made his way off the pitch, he felt a hand on his shoulder. He turned to come face-to-face with Pep Guardiola.

"You did well out there, kid," he said. "You've got a big future in this game."

Bernardo just stood there open-mouthed, not quite sure what to say, before muttering some mumbled thanks. Then, before he knew it, Pep was gone.

It was a tiny moment, but one that Bernardo would not forget easily. The best manager in the world knew who he was.

The second leg, at home, went even better for Monaco. They beat City 3-1 and sailed through on away goals.

Pep didn't come up and speak to Bernardo after that game.

Monaco continued to fly high on all fronts, knocking German titans Borussia Dortmund out 6-3 on aggregate in the Champions League quarter-finals, and flying to the top of the league.

In the Champions League semi-finals, they drew Italian champions Juventus, the team that had knocked them out in last season's Champions League. And, for the first time, they found a team that they couldn't break down.

Monaco were dumped out without scoring and, from a position where they looked as if they might be competing for four trophies, they were now down to just one – the league.

"We don't drop this now, boys, not when we're this close," Falcao warned, after a 3-1 win at home against Toulouse.

"Let's make sure we win this trophy, lads. It might be our last chance!" João Moutinho told the players.

There was a good chance that a number of Monaco's stars might be leaving the club at the end of the season. Bernardo, Fabinho and Kylian had all been linked with some of the biggest clubs across Europe, so this really might be the last chance for the current team to secure a trophy.

Four more wins would guarantee the title.

Then it was three.

Then two.

Then, on the final day of the season, against St-Étienne, only one. Monaco were three points clear of PSG, who also had just one game left to play. A win for Monaco today would seal the title.

The players could hear the fans partying before the game had even started.

"This is it, guys," Jardim said calmly before kick-off. "This is what we've been working for all season. When I see you in this changing room in 90 minutes, I want you to be here with the trophy!"

After 20 minutes, they got the perfect start. Young Kylian Mbappé got through, rounded the keeper and tucked the ball into an empty net.

A 1-0 lead was precarious, and Monaco knew that they needed to get a second goal to seal it.

After what seemed like hours, it finally came. Valère Germain tucked in the second goal, in the 91st minute of the match.

"Championes, championes, ole ole ole!" Bernardo yelled, as the team celebrated. It hadn't been Bernardo's finest game, but it didn't matter. Monaco were league champions for the first time since 2000, and they'd done it by beating the giants, PSG. For all of PSG's money and finances, Monaco had done the unthinkable.

Bernardo finished the league season with eight goals and nine assists. Unlike when Benfica had won the league, he really felt as if he'd contributed to the team's success, and he wore his medal proudly.

"What next?" Fabinho said to Bernardo, as they rested after the match. After the high adrenaline rush of the season, both players were completely exhausted, as if it had all hit them at once.

"Confederations Cup for me," Bernardo replied, his mind already on the next tournament. "And then, who knows?" he shrugged.

12
NEW CLUB, NEW COUNTRY

August 2017, Etihad Campus, Manchester, England

"I can't turn down the opportunity to play for Pep, can I?" Bernardo said to his agent. "Is there an offer on the table?"

"I know Monaco want about 50 million," his agent replied.

Bernardo's eyes widened. He didn't know what to say. 50 million was a ridiculous amount. Four years ago, he couldn't even get in the Benfica B-team. Nobody was going to pay that.

Monaco's title win had been one of the great underdog stories of the season, overcoming the might of PSG to take the French title.

But there was a suspicion in the media – and amongst some of the players – that it was little more than an underdog story. This didn't feel like the beginning of a new dynasty – it felt more like a one-off.

Bernardo had loved his time in Monaco. He loved the city, the manager and his team-mates. But he also had his own ambitions. He wanted to win more trophies, and he knew he wasn't going to do that at Monaco.

It was time to move.

As it turned out, Pep Guardiola had been so impressed by Bernardo that he'd been sniffing around with interest ever since Monaco had knocked City out of the Champions League.

"Look, Bernardo," his agent continued, "I don't want to get your hopes up, but I'm pretty certain that, this time next week, you'll be a Manchester City player."

"Wow," Bernardo sighed. Man City were a huge

team in England and, although they hadn't won the league in a few years, he knew that under Pep they'd be competing for the title *and* the Champions League.

His agent was right, and everything moved quickly after that. City ended up paying 45 million for Bernardo and he was soon on his way to Manchester to sign his contract.

"I'm thrilled you're here. We're going to achieve big things together," Pep told him, as he met Bernardo for the first time as a City player.

"I hope so!" Bernardo replied, as the pair shook hands and posed for photographs.

Bernardo immediately put on his boots to join the rest of the team for his first training session. He watched as De Bruyne fired in crosses for Sergio Agüero, who smashed them into the top corner every time.

During a break in the session, Sergio walked over to Bernardo to say hello.

"You're probably feeling a bit overwhelmed," Sergio said with a grin. "I was, when I first started here."

"Yeah. And I'm not even sure where I'm going to play," Bernardo replied.

"What do you mean?" Sergio asked.

"They've already got De Bruyne, David Silva, Sterling, Sané, Gündoğan, Yaya Toure … Where do I fit into that?"

"I'm sure they've signed you for a reason, bro. Just relax," Sergio laughed.

Throughout the training session, Pep stood on the sidelines, shouting instructions and acting out every action with his hands.

Bernardo could tell that Pep demanded 100% effort from every player in every session. If he wanted to find a place in Guardiola's team, he would have to work a lot harder than he'd done at Benfica or at Monaco.

Bernardo was right to be concerned. He featured in most City games, but it was almost always from the bench, often for just the last five or ten minutes, when the game was already won.

"I'm sorry to keep doing this, Bernardo," Pep conceded, after yet another game when Bernardo had barely featured. "We're on a really good run of form, and it's hard to rotate the side without losing momentum," Pep continued, and he seemed genuinely apologetic.

"That's OK," Bernardo said.

He meant it honestly. He was still adapting to English life – the language, the weather and the food – and he was still learning from all the players around him.

For the moment, he was happy to be able to adapt at his own pace, without a huge spotlight on him. He'd seen how harsh the English press could be to new signings, and he didn't particularly want that pressure until he felt settled.

He was now playing for what might be the best club in the world. He knew that he'd need to be at his very best to secure a place in the team.

13
FIRST OF MANY

February 2018, Wembley, London, England
League Cup Final, Manchester City v Arsenal

"You work harder than any other player in my team," Pep told Bernardo after one training session, perhaps sensing his new signing's concerns.

"I haven't seen anyone who will be sprinting towards the opposition box one minute and then, a second later, I see you pop up on the edge of our box, heading the ball clear! Incredible!" Pep continued.

Pep's enthusiasm and passion for the game was infectious. Every City player put 100% into every match, desperate to impress their manager and win points for him. This was how they felt, going into the final of the League Cup.

"This is the chance for our first trophy of the year," Pep told the players in the dressing room. "It sets the tone for the rest of the year. So let's make sure we win it, and make sure it's not the last one we win!"

To Bernardo's disappointment, he was on the bench for the game. Pep loved to tinker and change the team from game to game, in order to have the best chance of beating each opponent. Bernardo was the victim of that today, with De Bruyne, David Silva and Leroy Sané chosen to start instead.

City took an early lead after 18 minutes, through a brilliant Sergio Agüero finish that lobbed the keeper.

"Come on!" Bernardo shouted from the bench, joining in the celebrations.

City were comfortably maintaining their lead, but Fernandinho picked up a knock as the second half began.

Pep turned straight to Bernardo.

"Just keep the ball and don't let them get a sniff," Pep said to him on the touchline.

Five minutes later, Vincent Kompany poked City into a 2-0 lead, and barely 10 minutes after that it was three, when David Silva fired home.

"That's got to be game won now," Bernardo turned to De Bruyne. "They're not coming back from that, surely."

"Let's keep focused, still," De Bruyne replied. "No risks."

The game continued in the same fashion, with City holding onto the ball, not letting Arsenal get a touch.

Then, at last, the game was done. It hadn't been the most exciting of finals, but Bernardo and the City players didn't care.

"You've got one night off, lads, but don't get too crazy," Pep warned them, after they'd collected their medals. "We've still got a couple more trophies that I want us to win."

14
TITLE

April 2018, Anfield, Liverpool, England
UEFA Champions League, Liverpool v Manchester City

"You ever seen anything like this?" Bernardo asked De Bruyne, above the sound of the Liverpool fans banging on the sides of the City bus.

"Nah," the Belgian shrugged, "but the fans won't be on the pitch. We don't need to worry about them."

"I guess," Bernardo replied, wishing he could share De Bruyne's calmness.

With the League Cup in the bag and City a long way clear in the Premier League, the focus turned to the Champions League. City had been drawn against Liverpool in the quarter-finals – the only team who had beaten them in the Premier League so far.

The first leg was at Anfield, and the City bus was being greeted by flares and thousands of jeering and howling Liverpool fans. The bus was barely able to make it through the crowds, and the City players could all feel the Liverpool fans banging on the sides of the bus.

Bernardo had a feeling that this wasn't going to be quite as easy a game as De Bruyne thought. During the warm-up, he occasionally glanced across at the Liverpool players. They looked more determined and focused than any group of players he'd seen.

Once more, Bernardo was the victim of Pep's tinkering, and he spent the whole game on the bench. He ended up completely frustrated as Liverpool ran out comfortable 3-0 winners. It was a thrashing, and City's Champions League hopes were in tatters.

"What happened out there?" Bernardo murmured to Leroy Sané, after the game.

"They just outran us," Leroy sighed, clearly not wanting to talk about it.

The return leg was six days later, back at the Etihad. City knew that it was going to be a huge ask to score three goals, especially because Pep knew that Liverpool were at their most dangerous on the counter-attack, with Salah, Mané and Firmino.

"You've just got to go for it, OK guys?" Pep said. "Nothing more to it. If we lose, we lose. You can do nothing wrong today, as long as you try."

Bernardo was glad to be back in the starting line-up for the big game. He could feel the adrenaline pumping through him as the players lined up in the tunnel. He was sure that they could overturn the defeat. He'd done the impossible before, with Monaco, and he felt confident he could do it again tonight.

Within minutes of kick-off, van Dijk made a mistake and Sterling was played in behind. He squared the ball to Gabriel Jesus, who beat the keeper to score.

The noise from the City fans was deafening. Suddenly, they had an extra level of belief that their team could do this.

"Two more, boys!" The shout came from David Silva, but he hadn't needed to say anything – they all knew what they had to do.

The game proved to be frustrating, with chances going wide, a goal disallowed and passes going astray. At half-time, City still had the one-goal lead.

Pep didn't say anything in the dressing room. The players didn't need motivating or instructing – they knew what they needed to do.

The second half was even more frustrating, as Liverpool equalised early.

Then, 15 minutes later, Bernardo was subbed off. He slumped into his seat in despair. He knew he'd been disappointing tonight – and now City were out of the Champions League.

But the disappointment didn't last long.

Five days later, it was all forgotten, as City were declared Premier League champions.

"That's two league titles in two years!" Bernardo shouted to Agüero, as they celebrated. "I thought it was supposed to be hard!"

This season, City weren't just *any* champions – they

were record-breakers. By the time the season had finished, they'd amassed a record 100 points.

Without doubt, they were one of the best teams of all time.

"How'd you enjoy your first season in England, then, Bernardo?" Vincent Kompany asked him, as they enjoyed the celebrations.

Bernardo paused.

"Not bad!" he grinned, "but I don't think I played my best, really. I feel like I can do so much more next year."

"Don't worry about it," Kompany replied. "Everybody struggles the first season. To be honest with you, I think you've played brilliantly – you're already a key part of the team."

"Thanks," Bernardo said. "I just hope I haven't exhausted myself before the World Cup."

15
ONE DOWN, FOUR TO GO

August 2018, Wembley, London, England
Chelsea v Manchester City

"Cristiano's got this," Bernardo said to the other substitutes.

Portugal were playing Spain, in their first World Cup group match, in a group that included Spain, Iran and Morocco.

Bernardo had played the first 70 minutes of the game, but he was shattered after his long season with

City and he'd been subbed off. He'd been forced to look on as Spain had taken a 3-2 lead.

Then, in the last minute, Portugal won a free-kick and it was Ronaldo who stepped up to whip the ball into the top corner, to seal his hat-trick. Portugal had snatched a draw, and it felt like a great start to the tournament.

Portugal went on to win the next game, against Morocco, before slumping to a draw against Iran.

"We've done OK, lads," the manager said, as they prepared for the last-16 game against Uruguay. "But we need to step up to the level we were playing at during Euro 2016, if we want to go far in this tournament."

He was right, but Portugal struggled to compete with Uruguay. Cavani, a man who had haunted Bernardo during his time at Monaco, scored twice, and Portugal were out before they'd even had an opportunity to begin.

"I'm like a curse to this side, man," Bernardo moaned. "We never win when I'm in the team."

Nobody was in the mood to disagree with him. Once more, Bernardo found himself on a coach full of silent players. He'd never felt more desperate to be back in England with Man City.

In fact, Bernardo was concerned about his return to City. They had already dipped into the transfer market, signing a new right-winger in Riyad Mahrez.

"This must mean I'm out of the team, then," Bernardo complained to Vincent Kompany.

"Of course not, Bernardo. Don't be stupid," Vincent said. "He's just adding squad depth. Maybe the boss will play you in the centre or something."

The first match of the season was the Community Shield, the annual clash between the Premier League winners and the FA Cup winners. City were up against Chelsea, but both clubs were missing a number of players who had gone far into the World Cup.

"We win this and we get our first trophy of the season," Pep said. "We lay down a marker and we say to the rest of the country, 'We are Man City and we're not going anywhere.'"

Bernardo had half-expected to start the game on the bench but, to his surprise, he was chosen to start, alongside Leroy Sané and Riyad Mahrez.

"I want you somewhere a bit different today, OK Bernardo?" Pep told him before the game. "I want you in midfield – where David plays. Create chances, create goals, keep the ball. OK?"

Bernardo nodded. He knew he was capable of playing in that deeper midfield role – he'd just never been asked to play there before.

The game started well for City, with Sergio Agüero firing them in front after just 13 minutes. The game was played at a slower pace than most Premier League games, but Bernardo tried to keep up the pace, maintain the pressure. Since Portugal's exit at the World Cup, he'd been desperate to get back on the pitch. He felt the need to atone for what he thought had been poor performances.

Fifteen minutes into the second half, Bernardo picked the ball up in his usual place on the right-hand side. He saw the run of Agüero and drifted inside, playing an inch-perfect pass. Agüero didn't need a second invitation to unleash his shot.

GOAL!

"Great pass, mate. Would have fooled me for David Silva!" Sergio joked to Bernardo as they celebrated.

The game was done by that point. Chelsea were

missing their talisman, Eden Hazard, and both teams were struggling in the heat.

The win was confirmed a few minutes later. City had another trophy.

"That's one down, four to go," Bernardo said to Sterling, as they put their medals around their necks.

After the disappointment of the World Cup, Bernardo was more determined than ever to have the best season of his career with City, and to win every available trophy.

16
THE STUFF OF DREAMS

February 2019, Wembley, London, England
Carabao Cup Final, Chelsea v Manchester City

"In all the time I've been playing with you, I had no idea you could finish like that!" David Silva joked with Bernardo during a training session.

"Neither did I," Bernardo chuckled.

Bernardo's new level of determination hadn't gone unnoticed by his team-mates or by his manager. Bernardo didn't feel as if he'd improved as a footballer –

it was just that he had a new mentality. Now, he wanted to win everything.

His form continued into the new season, scoring on the opening day against Arsenal with a powerful driving effort into the top corner. That was the goal that had made David Silva look at him with fresh eyes.

In the space of just six months, Bernardo had gone from being a bit-part player at City, playing only 10 or 15 minutes in a game, to being an integral part of the side. He usually played the full 90 minutes in most matches now – Pep had no choice but to start him.

"I don't know what's happened to you, Bernardo," Pep said, shaking his head in disbelief. "You're like a man possessed, this season."

Bernardo shrugged. He didn't have any answers – he just knew that he wanted to do everything he could to make sure that City took home the title once more.

Bernardo had also racked up more miles in games than any other player that season. To many, he never seemed to tire.

"How do you run so much?" Agüero asked him, after one match.

"I'm not sure," Bernardo said. "I just want to get the ball and keep it – and I want to get it to our guys."

"And that's all it takes?" Agüero gave him a strange look. "You're not doing a load of extra work in the gym, are you?"

"Does it really look like I am?" Bernardo laughed.

Bernardo had certainly come a long way since Benfica. His work ethic had been an issue there, and it had been the main reason why Jorge Jesus had told Bernardo he wouldn't make it.

Pep saw Bernardo's new work ethic as his biggest quality. He could win the ball back high up the pitch, before the opposition could trouble City's defence. And he didn't just win the ball back – he would then do something with it. He could create chances and even score himself.

Bernardo's defensive instincts came to the fore during City's second consecutive League Cup final. They were up against Chelsea at Wembley once more – but this time, it was a much more hard-fought game.

It wasn't a game of skill or beautiful passing, so much as a tough midfield battle, with Bernardo at the centre of it. He tussled and fought with the Chelsea midfield, battling for every ball.

When the time came for Pep to make his changes, it was David Silva and Kevin De Bruyne that he took off. He needed Bernardo out there.

That kind of support gave Bernardo further inspiration, and he found an extra gear as the game went into extra time. Then, finally, it went to penalties.

"Who's taking, then?" Pep asked, looking around at his group of exhausted players. They had an assigned list, but sometimes players couldn't do it on the day – either due to sheer exhaustion, or because they were too nervous.

Bernardo put his hand up straight away.

"I'll have one," he said.

He'd missed the opportunity to take penalties for Portugal before, and had been forced to watch helplessly as his team lost. He wasn't letting that happen today.

Bernardo was fourth on the list for City and, when it came to him, Luiz had missed for Chelsea and Leroy Sané had seen his effort saved. Bernardo could put City 3-2 up.

He breathed out deeply and looked at the Chelsea keeper. He had an idea of where he was going to put it, but it was very different now that he was up there, on the spot.

Bernardo glanced at the fans behind the goal, then turned his eyes back to the ball. That was all that mattered right now. Then he took a few steps and smashed the ball hard down the middle, watching the keeper fly to his left.

"No drama," he smiled, as he jogged back to the half-way line.

A few minutes later, it was the job of Raheem Sterling to win it for City. He needn't have worried. Raheem smashed it high into the top left-hand corner.

City had their second trophy of the season!

"Bernardo! Bernardo!" Pep called, pulling him over. "You're Man of the Match, OK? They need you to collect your award! Well played today!"

Bernardo couldn't believe it. Scoring a penalty, winning a cup final, *and* getting Man of the Match.

It was the stuff of dreams.

17
UP FOR THE QUADRUPLE

April 2019, Etihad Stadium, Manchester, England
UEFA Champions League, Manchester City v Spurs

"Liverpool just won't let up, will they?" Sergio Agüero moaned.

Agüero was a veteran of three title wins with City, but even he seemed concerned by just how well Liverpool were doing.

"We've just got to keep winning," Pep replied. "It doesn't matter what they do, OK?"

City were still in the middle of a tense title race, and Liverpool were hot on their heels, just a point behind. On top of that, there was still the Champions League and the FA Cup, and City were desperate to win all three remaining competitions.

Pep wanted City to keep on winning, and that's exactly what they did, with some wins proving memorable – a 6-0 win over Chelsea in the league, a 3-2 comeback win away at Swansea in the FA Cup, and a 7-0 thrashing of Schalke in the Champions League.

"This season is going down in history," Bernardo said to Raheem, after they had advanced into the semi-finals of the FA Cup. "We're going to win everything."

"Easy, Bernardo," Raheem replied. "One step at a time. We might do the quadruple, but we might end it all with just one trophy."

In the Champions League, City were facing English rivals Tottenham Hotspur in the quarter-finals. Bernardo was injured for the first leg, and had to watch from the sidelines as they were beaten 1-0 away from home.

Bernardo was fit for the second leg, but he was

nervous. He couldn't shake the feeling that this was going to be just like Liverpool last season. City were going to be knocked out by an English club once again.

The City fans were in good voice for the game, and they were quickly given something to cheer when, after barely four minutes, Raheem Sterling whipped a shot into the back of the net.

"We're level! Now let's go and win this thing!" Pep roared from the sidelines, urging his players to get a quick second goal.

Then, in the space of just seven minutes, the game turned on its head once more. Heung-min Son scored twice in quick succession for Spurs, giving them a 2-1 lead – and, more importantly, two crucial away goals.

"How did that happen?" Bernardo murmured to himself. He was determined to do something about it.

He picked the ball up on his usual right-hand side, driving at the left-back, Danny Rose. He forced him back and then let fly, aiming to curl the ball into the far corner. It deflected off Rose, but fooled the keeper and snuck in at the near post.

Now it was 2-2.

"That's mine!" Bernardo roared, urging the players back to the half-way line to restart the game. They still needed two more goals.

Ten minutes later, City had a third. De Bruyne fired in a cross and Raheem Sterling emerged at the back post to tuck it home.

Half-time came and went with the score still at 3-2. City still needed another goal.

Fifteen minutes into the second half, the ball found Sergio Agüero. One chance was all he needed and he smashed it into the top corner. City had the lead.

"Let's keep this now, lads," Bernardo shouted.

Fifteen minutes later, there was another twist. Fernando Llorente bundled the ball home from a corner for Spurs. Bernardo saw the appeals from his team-mates for handball but, despite the presence of VAR, the goal stood.

Once more, City were staring down the barrel of defeat.

With 90 minutes on the clock, the ball bounced forward, into the path of Agüero. He slipped it to Sterling, who went past one defender and fired a shot.

The ball beat the keeper and hit the back of the net.

GOAL!

City had done it! In the most unbelievable comeback, they were through to the Champions League semi-finals.

As the team celebrated, Bernardo spotted the ref speaking to the video referees. There was going to be a VAR check.

The announcement came over the tannoy first. The goal had been disallowed for offside.

For City, the Champions League – and the quadruple dream – was over.

18
TROPHIES

June 2019, Estádio do Dragão, Porto, Portugal
UEFA Nations League Final, Portugal v Netherlands

"We're not relaxing yet, lads," Pep warned the team. "We've got an FA Cup final to win."

City's title fight with Liverpool had gone right to the final day of the season, with City winning 4-1 against Brighton, to secure a second consecutive Premier League title, beating Liverpool by one point.

But any thoughts of taking it easy after the title

win were scuppered by Pep, who intended to keep the pressure up.

If the Premier League title race had been a war, the FA Cup final was barely a scuffle. City had expected a challenge from Watford, but Watford were off their game – and City were on top of theirs.

Two goals each for Gabriel Jesus and Raheem Sterling were accompanied by goals for De Bruyne and David Silva, as City ran out emphatic 6-0 winners.

Bernardo, De Bruyne and David Silva had all been at the centre of it, in the heart of that midfield. They were simply untouchable.

"Enjoy the break, lads," Pep reminded the players, as they prepared to go their separate ways at the end of the season. "We're going to do it all over again next year – and, next year, we *will* get that Champions League!"

"I'll see you in Portugal, Bernardo," Raheem Sterling said to him, as they walked out of the training ground together.

"Only if you win your semi-final," Bernardo corrected him with a grin.

Both England and Portugal were in the semi-finals of

the new Nations League competition, which was taking place in Portugal this summer.

Bernardo was desperate to win a trophy with his country, and he didn't see a better opportunity than the Nations League.

Portugal's semi-final was against Switzerland. They weren't expected to be tough opposition, but Bernardo remembered João Moutinho's advice from all those years ago. You could never tell at international level.

It took 25 minutes before the deadlock was broken, and there was no shock about who was responsible. Cristiano Ronaldo, Portugal's captain and arguably the best player in the world, scored from a stunning free kick. The roar of the home crowd was deafening.

"Let's get a second now, boys," Cristiano roared, as they celebrated the goal. Coming from him, it sounded like an order.

In the second half, Bernardo was victim to more VAR drama. He was brought down in the Swiss box and it looked to be a clear penalty – an opportunity for Ronaldo to get his second.

But it wasn't to be.

The referee checked the cameras and decided that Switzerland should have had a penalty at the other end. Ricardo Rodriguez duly put it away and now it was 1-1.

Game back on.

The game was quiet and tense, and it looked as if it was fizzling out to extra time and penalties.

Then, with minutes left, the ball was crossed in towards Bernardo. It drifted in the air, but he was able to bring it down. He looked up, spotting the run of Cristiano, and eased it into his path. Ronaldo did the rest, blasting it past the keeper.

Portugal were back in the lead.

"Great pass, Bernardo!" Cristiano shouted. "Let's see this game out now."

But there was more to come. As Switzerland pushed forward, Portugal broke. Ronaldo got the ball, cut inside and smashed it into the net.

It was 3-1 to Portugal – and a hat-trick for Ronaldo.

In the final, Portugal faced not England, but the Netherlands, captained by Virgil van Dijk.

"I've spent my whole year stopping van Dijk from winning a trophy. I'm certainly not going to let him have one now," Bernardo said to Moutinho, before the game.

Again, it was a tough game. Both teams were evenly matched, finding it difficult to break each other down.

After just under an hour of football, Bernardo got the ball and burst into the box. In the corner of his eye he saw van Dijk coming towards him – but he also saw Gonçalo Guedes. He flicked the ball back to Guedes, who took one touch and then whipped it into the bottom corner.

Portugal were leading in the final.

"Come on!" Bernardo roared, sprinting after Guedes in celebration. He was desperate to get his hands on a trophy with Portugal.

The minutes seemed to tick by like hours but, at last, it happened. The ref blew the final whistle. Portugal had won the Nations League Cup – and Bernardo could collect his medal.

"I can't believe it's finally happened," he said to João Moutinho, as they enjoyed the celebrations.

"You deserve it, bro," Moutinho replied. "You know I always used to say, 'We'll be alright, we've got

Cristiano', but now it's different. Now I say, 'We'll be alright, we've got Cristiano AND Bernardo.'"

Bernardo laughed, but he wasn't sure about the Cristiano comparisons just yet. There was still one trophy he needed. The Champions League. And he wasn't stopping until he got that.

19
MORE FRUSTRATION

August 2020, Estádio José Alvalade, Lisbon, Portugal
UEFA Champions League, Olympique Lyonnais v Man City

"We're away in one of the biggest stadiums in the world," Pep told his players. "We win this and we send out a message to the rest of Europe – we're here to be Champions of Europe."

Bernardo had been nominated as one of the 30 candidates to win the Ballon d'Or, after his outstanding 2019, and City had ended the previous season on a high with a domestic treble. But since then it had been a downward spiral. They'd had a poor start to the season and had slipped well behind runaway leaders Liverpool in the Premier League.

By January, the title race was all but over, and City had turned their attentions to the other competitions. They were in the League Cup final – and they had a huge last-16 Champions League tie against Real Madrid.

Keen to send a message out to the rest of Europe, Guardiola was in a typically demanding mood before the Real Madrid game.

Bernardo had won everything he could with City, except for the Champions League – the one trophy that had always stayed just out of reach. The disappointment of last year still loomed large in his mind.

As usual, Pep had tinkered with the structure of the team, to try to spring a surprise on Real Madrid. Bernardo was starting up front with team-mate Kevin De Bruyne just behind him, and normal striker Gabriel Jesus out on the left.

"They won't be expecting you up there, Bernardo,"

Pep told him before the game. "Drag them around a bit, drop deep and get the ball, keep finding pockets of space. They will struggle."

Pep's words proved to be prophetic. Real Madrid struggled with City's new-look formation and, although they took the lead, Bernardo always felt confident.

Indeed, City did turn it around, winning 2-1. It was a famous win against one of the biggest clubs in Europe, and surely set the tone for a real run at the Champions League trophy.

A week later, Bernardo was lifting yet another domestic trophy with City, as they won the League Cup in front of a packed Wembley crowd.

Perhaps the season wasn't going to be quite so bad after all.

Then, not long after City had won the League Cup, the whole season was called off. The COVID-19 pandemic had brought the season to a crushing halt and, for three months, the City players were locked down at home, trying as best they could to keep in form and stay fit.

Eventually, the season resumed but, with the title

gone, the rest of the Premier League season was of little interest to City. All they cared about was the Champions League.

Because some countries were suffering from COVID-19 more than others, UEFA decided that the remaining Champions League games would be played over a few weeks in Portugal.

After a comfortable 2-1 win in the second leg over Real Madrid, City faced their next challenge – a quarter-final against Lyon.

Not surprisingly, City were huge favourites.

"It's going to be a different test for us today," Pep explained. "I want a slightly different formation, something to allow us to control the match."

He'd gone for a 3-5-2 formation, and there was no space in that setup for Bernardo. Unusually, he was starting on the bench.

At half-time, City were 1-0 down.

"I've got to get out there," Bernardo complained to David Silva, sitting next to him. "We both should be out there."

In the second half, City pulled a goal back through

Kevin De Bruyne, and it looked as if they were back on track to get into the semi-finals.

But then everything fell apart.

Laporte made an error at the back, which allowed Moussa Dembélé to score for Lyon, putting them 2-1 up.

City wasted chance after chance as they looked for an equaliser. Sterling even missed a wide-open goal, by blazing the ball over the bar from inside the six-yard box.

Bernardo looked over to Pep. Surely he had to bring him on?

Then, on Lyon's next attack, Ederson spilled a save, and Dembélé was there to tap in the rebound and make it 3-1.

Once more, Bernardo looked over at Pep, but he didn't summon him from the bench.

Bernardo watched in frustration as City were beaten 3-1 by Lyon, once more getting dumped out of the Champions League at the quarter-finals.

Bernardo was going to finish the season with only a League Cup trophy to his name.

20
WITHIN GRASP?

February 2021, Puskás Aréna, Budapest, Hungary
UEFA Champions League, Borussia Mönchengladbach
v Manchester City

Bernardo returned to City at the start of the 2020-21 season to find a renewed vigour around the squad. Pep had recruited Rúben Dias as the new centre-back and Ferran Torres had joined them further forward.

Pep seemed more confident than Bernardo had ever seen him.

"We had a poor year last year, lads," Pep announced.

"But it won't be happening again. You want your title back, don't you?"

The players all nodded.

"Then you will have to fight for it," he continued. "And not just for the title, but for everything else. We want to be record-breakers and history-makers. We want to win everything."

"Do you think we can?" João Cancelo whispered to Bernardo, as they watched Pep.

"Why not?" Bernardo shrugged. "We're good enough."

But it seemed that Pep had been too confident. City struggled during the early part of the season and, after a 2-0 defeat to Tottenham, they found themselves in tenth place in the league. Hopes of any trophy – let alone a quadruple – now seemed far out of reach.

But then things clicked, and suddenly City were winning. A 3-1 win at Chelsea, 5-0 at West Brom, 4-1 against Liverpool, 3-0 against Spurs … City weren't just doing well – they were flying. Now there wasn't a team that could touch them.

It wasn't just in the Premier League that City were

on form. They were into another League Cup final, and they had eased through their group in the Champions League. *And* they were in the FA Cup semi-finals.

Pep had been right. They really could win it all.

The next game was a big one. It was away to Borussia Mönchengladbach in the Champions League. This was the competition that Bernardo was desperate to win. He needed to make amends for all the years where this competition had ended badly for him.

City went into the match on an 18-game winning streak in all competitions. It was unprecedented to go so many games without losing, let alone to win all of them.

"I'm not losing it tonight," Bernardo declared defiantly to Raheem Sterling. "We are *not* going to lose this!"

"I'm looking out for you tonight," João Cancelo suddenly announced. "When was the last time you scored, Bernardo? You need to start pulling your weight!"

"Hey!" Bernardo protested, turning to see a grinning Cancelo jogging out onto the pitch.

With just under half an hour played, Cancelo lived

up to his promise. He got the ball just outside the box and floated a beautiful ball into the area. Bernardo had seen it coming and he raced towards it, nipping in behind the defender without being spotted.

The ball was weighted perfectly for a header, and Bernardo guided it into the far corner of the goal.

He turned and pointed to Cancelo, thanking his friend for the cross.

"That was brilliant, João," he said.

"I thought you'd miss," Cancelo replied. "I mean, when was the last time you scored with your head?"

"If you keep doing crosses like that, I'll get a few more," Bernardo laughed, as the two celebrated the goal.

City didn't get a second until the second half. Once more, it was a beautiful cross from Cancelo. And once more, Bernardo had snuck around the back behind the defender.

This time, he couldn't direct it towards goal himself, but he saw Gabriel Jesus making a run into the box.

He nodded the ball back towards Jesus, allowing the striker to tap it in.

"Didn't fancy a second?" Cancelo laughed, as he joined the celebrations.

"The ball wasn't good enough this time," Bernardo replied.

City were in control for the rest of the game, and ran out comfortable 2-0 winners.

They had now won 19 consecutive games, and the quadruple was again in their sights.

"This is our year, Bernardo. I really believe it. Are you with me?" Pep said to Bernardo in the dressing room after the game.

"Always, boss," Bernardo replied, as he hugged his manager.

Bernardo wanted to win everything, but more than anything else, he wanted the Champions League. He'd reached the quarter-finals so many times before, but this year, Bernardo felt closer to winning the competition than ever before.

As he looked around the changing room at Pep and his team-mates, he thought back to his childhood years. Back then, when he'd been kicking a ball about as a boy in Lisbon, who would have thought he'd end up here, in the dressing room of the world's greatest club?

I belong here, Bernardo thought to himself. *This is my time.*

21
MY TIME

June 2023, Atatürk Olympic Stadium, Istanbul, Turkey
UEFA Champions League Final, Man City v Inter Milan

Bernardo had been sure that in the 2020-21 season City would win it all. They'd seemed unstoppable – and in the Premier League they had been, storming to the title with a 12-point margin over second-place Man United.

Even so, Bernardo had been disappointed with his lack of game time in the second half of the season.

All too often, he'd found himself sitting on the bench, watching his team win games without him.

City had also won the League Cup, beating Spurs 1-0 in the final. But once again, Bernardo had played for just a measly three minutes, only coming off the bench at the end of the match.

He'd then had to watch from the sidelines as City were beaten by Chelsea in the FA Cup semi-finals. This was becoming a frustrating pattern for Bernardo. It seemed to him that, no matter what he did, he couldn't get any decent game time in the matches that counted.

But the worst moment had come in the Champions League – the very tournament that Bernardo was most desperate to win.

City had made it all the way to the final, where they were once again facing Chelsea. Bernardo had started the game, but had been subbed off after an hour, with City trailing 1-0.

The game ended without further goals, making Chelsea the champions of Europe. City had lost in the Champions League final – and Bernardo had been forced to watch the last third of the game helplessly from the bench.

The season had left Bernardo feeling doubtful about his future at City. With so many great players in the team, he couldn't be sure there was a place for him any longer.

After the end of the season, he'd been linked with a move away from Manchester, with rumours that historic clubs like Atlético Madrid and A.C. Milan were showing interest in signing him.

While he'd still been thinking about his options, Pep had called him into his office for a meeting.

Pep knew his players well, and he'd seen how Bernardo had seemed distracted recently in training. He'd wanted to know why.

"So, you've heard the rumours about Atlético and A.C. Milan?" Pep had asked. "These are two great clubs – I can see why their interest would be attractive."

"They're both offering me a long contract, boss. I'm nearly 27 now – maybe it's time for me to move on," Bernardo had said quietly, seeing no point in trying to hide his thoughts from Pep.

"You are vital to this team, Bernardo," Pep had answered bluntly. "I want you to stay at City."

Bernardo had looked at Pep in surprise. City had so many great players, so what difference would his leaving make?

"These other players are superstars, it is true. Everyone talks about Kevin De Bruyne, about Erling, about our attacking players – but you are always under the radar. It is one of your best assets. If some people don't notice you, it is their fault. I know how much of a difference you make to my team."

Pep had gazed across at Bernardo, catching his eye. "If you stay, Bernardo, you will be a key member of the squad going forward."

After a lot of thought, Bernardo had decided to stay at City – at least to see out the rest of his contract.

Almost immediately, he'd realised that he'd made the right decision. Even though City *only* won the Premier League title in the season that followed – this time by just one point over Liverpool – for Bernardo, things had begun to change very quickly.

He'd become a key figure in the team, just as Pep

had said he would be. He was now playing almost every game in the league, and he'd also played in every game in the Champions League knockout stages.

The following season started with Bernardo fully committed to City and convinced that they could win every tournament they competed in.

City had gone on to win the Premier League for the third season in a row, beating Arsenal to the title by a five-point margin – with Bernardo again featuring in most of the games.

They'd then completed the double by winning the FA Cup, beating local rivals Man United 2-1, with Bernardo playing the full 90 minutes.

Best of all, the one trophy that Bernardo most wanted to win was once again in his sights. City had fought their way through to the Champions League final, where they would meet Inter Milan.

Bernardo felt sure that, this time, City would be lifting the trophy.

There was never a question of whether he'd be playing – he'd played in every Champions League game this season.

From the kick-off, Bernardo realised that Pep had been right about the way other teams saw him. The Inter Milan defenders seemed to be so worried about covering City's big stars – the likes of Erling Haaland, Kevin De Bruyne and Jack Grealish – that they simply overlooked Bernardo.

So, when on 68 minutes Bernardo made a run through the Inter Milan defence, he wasn't surprised to see that his run hadn't been tracked.

Manuel Akanji slid the ball into Bernardo's path, and he quickly turned and fizzed it back across the box. Rodri was the first to react, running onto the ball before smashing it into the net.

City had taken the lead in the Champions League final – thanks to an assist from Bernardo.

Inter Milan had no response to going behind and City saw the rest of the game out comfortably.

The full-time whistle saw Manchester City hailed as the new champions of Europe.

Bernardo had finally achieved a personal *treble* of his own. He'd made himself an indispensible part of Pep's first team, he'd won the Champions League trophy –

providing the assist that had secured the winning goal – and he'd helped City win the continental treble.

At the end of the game, the City players celebrated with their fans, before receiving the trophy that Bernardo had worked his whole career to hold.

As the players were making their way back to the dressing room after the medals ceremony, Erling Haaland caught up with Bernardo.

"Manchester City are European Champions! Can you believe it, Bernardo?" Erling Haaland asked, barely containing his excitement.

"Of course! We're the best team in the world – and we have you up front," Bernardo laughed.

"Hey, I didn't even score today, and you got the assist for Rodri. Looks like you might be the best playmaker in the world too," Erling grinned, before running off to celebrate with the trophy.

Bernardo looked down at the Champions League winner's medal hanging around his neck. He had finally done it. Without a doubt, this had to be the pinnacle of his career – at least, *so far*. He'd won many trophies with every club he'd played for, but none felt as special as this.

Bernardo reflected on how far he'd come with City since he'd almost left in 2021.

Now, he'd achieved everything he'd set out to do with the team.

He'd scored great goals, made important assists and had ultimately been the match-winner on countless occasions.

He'd become Pep's secret weapon, the player who flew under the radar, but could turn a game with a single pass or shot.

Pep had made it clear that there was a new contract waiting for Bernardo at City, if he wanted it. And now Bernardo knew that he did.

Manchester City was his home. Why would he go anywhere else?

He was still only 28 and had so much more to give. There was still plenty of time to create many more great memories with City.

He wasn't slowing down any time soon.

HOW MANY HAVE YOU READ?

- MESSI
- HAALAND
- RASHFORD
- SALAH
- KELLY
- SANCHO
- KANE
- LEWANDOWSKI
- NEYMAR
- MBAPPÉ
- SON
- KLOPP
- SAKA
- STERLING
- VAN DIJK
- SILVA
- MAHREZ
- GUARDIOLA
- GNABRY
- KANTÉ
- RONALDO
- PULISIC
- FÉLIX
- SOUTHGATE
- BELLINGHAM
- WIEGMAN